Curl Up And Die

A SADIE WEINSTEIN MYSTERY

REVA SPIRO LUXENBERG

authorHOUSE®

AuthorHouse™ LLC
1663 Liberty Drive
Bloomington, IN 47403
www.authorhouse.com
Phone: 1-800-839-8640

Published by AuthorHouse   04/14/2014

ISBN: 978-1-4969-0369-3 (sc)
ISBN: 978-1-4969-0370-9 (e)

Library of Congress Control Number: 2014907042

BOOKS BY
Reva Spiro Luxenberg

Sadie Weinstein Mysteries
Murder at the Second Lily Pond
The Cereal Killer
Curl Up and Die

*　　*　　*

Grand Army Plaza
And There Was Light
A Flickering Flame
The Call from Beyond and Other Stories
Native American Fun Crafts
Ari, the Ant
Pappy, the Puppy
Romantic Calligraphy
Chuckling with Reva, Volumes 1 & 2

DEDICATED TO THE MEMORY OF

Gary Provost, my teacher and mentor

ACKNOWLEDGMENT

In gratitude to my editor, Jill Herring

CHAPTER 1

I tucked my lavender panties in my suitcase as Nathan looked on. Sitting on the bed with his jeans unhooked and his basketball tummy popping out, his chocolate eagle eyes scrutinized my every move. I continued carefully packing the remainder of my pastel-colored panties. Our mom-and-pop grocery in Brooklyn would get along without us, as our clerk and my cousin, Bunny, would look after it. We deserved a vacation.

Two weeks before every trip we took, I began to pack, not like Nathan who started only two hours before. Once he had forgotten his toothbrush, which was no big deal, and once he left behind his sneakers, also no big deal, but when we took a Mexican cruise he forgot his hearing aids and bellyached when he couldn't hear the comedian at the show.

"Sadie?" he asked in his raspy voice.

"Yes?" I knew what was coming and I smirked.

"Why do we have to go to the Grand Canyon?"

"It's one of the wonders of the world. I get first pick because I won the money." I had helped the police solve the Cereal Killer case, the one in Brooklyn when the murderer had been shooting dope pushers and sprinkling cereal on their bodies. With the substantial sum of reward money, I modernized our mom-and-pop grocery, gave some to our grown children, and picked the place where we would vacation.

"Hmm," Nathan said. "It's only a big hole in the ground."

"It's amazing," I said cheerfully. "Before we pass on to the next world, we have to see it." I held up my Wonderbra and waved it in front of him. The bra was created in 1964, two years ago, and with its deep plunge and push-together effect, it made for a terrific view of my figure.

"I ain't of the same opinion," Nathan persisted.

This time, I realized, looking at my bra didn't change Nathan's mind, so I took a deep breath and put it in the suitcase next to my panties. Nathan is really very smart and knowledgeable, although his grammar makes him seem illiterate. I believe he does this on purpose so as not to show off. He's a really modest man. I'm proud to say that he finishes *The New York Times* crossword puzzle in ink.

"It's in the same category as the Leaning Tower of Pisa and Stonehenge," I said, hoping to change his mind, but deep inside I knew that when Nathan held on to an opinion, it stuck like rubber glue.

Nathan glared. "The Leaning Tower of Pisa ain't built right. It wouldn't lean if the architect had designed it properly, and ain't it true we stood and looked at Stonehenge when we went to England when you solved the mystery of who killed Jeffrey's professor? Everyone says that Stonehenge was a religious site, but everyone ain't right. There was a dry moat around it, and I say it held water for the animals, and Stonehenge was the first supermarket. Sadie, pretty lady, we already saw two wonders of the world, and don't forget an additional one, the Brooklyn Bridge, an industrial wonder. Since we work like beavers, ain't we entitled to relax, go fishing, and not travel across the country to see a hole in the ground?"

I can be stubborn, too. "No, maybe we can go fishing some other time but not . . ." The doorbell rang four times and stopped me from talking. It was ten o'clock at night and no one comes to our door so late. It must be an emergency or someone up to no good. "I have on my nightgown," I said. "You go answer and make sure you look through the peephole before you open the door."

I threw on my chenille bathrobe and followed Nathan through the living room to the foyer of our four-room apartment. Nathan looked through the peephole.

"It's Don," he said.

I pulled the belt of my robe tight and shivered when our neighbor, Don Morris, walked through the door. His usually dapper appearance had dissolved into chaos. His corn-colored hair was disheveled, there was no tie at the open collar of his shirt, and his expression looked like he had been to Hades and back. Immediately, I thought that Dolly had tried once again to commit suicide. Three years ago their only child, a boy of twelve, had been in a fatal accident when a car had smashed into his bike. Dolly had fallen into a deep depression and had turned the gas on in the kitchen, but Don had come home unexpectedly and saved her. She was still keeping pretty much to herself, but somehow Don had gone on living, coping by taking frequent business trips to promote his beauty products.

Don followed Nathan to the living room where they both sat down on our sofa with the clear plastic covers that protected the damask print. I reclined on my low armchair so I could rest my feet on our worn Oriental rug. I'm not quite five feet, so high chairs aren't for me.

"What's wrong?" I asked Don.

My neighbor took a deep breath, pursing his thin lips, and letting the air out slowly. My sky blue eyes remained glued on him.

"Dolly's been weeping again. I'm worried about her grip on reality. She isolates herself and has stopped cooking. She buys only TV dinners."

"Have you spoken to her doctor?" Nathan asked with a worried expression.

"Yes. Her psychiatrist recommended a change of environment to lift her mood. I planned on going to the beauty academy in Miami Beach to display my new line of head mannequins and wigs. I also sell my merchandise to the beauty parlors and beauty supply stores in the South so I'll be traveling a little. It took me a long time to convince Dolly to fly to Florida. The catch is she won't go without you. I get a good deal at an exclusive hotel, the Gold Coast Suites, which is close to the beauty school, the one I do business with. It's inexpensive since the students learn by practicing on customers who like to save money."

Don raised his blond eyebrows as he looked expectantly at me.

"I'm sorry that Dolly's so low, but you know that we're leaving for the Grand Canyon on July 15th. Our reservations are in. Everything's arranged. We couldn't possibly go with you. I'm really sorry, but it's out of the question."

Don spoke up. "You and Dolly could go to the beauty school every day while Nathan and I go deep sea fishing when I'm not busy selling my merchandise."

"I don't think so," I said raising my voice. "I already told everyone we're going to the Grand Canyon. I told my kids, my cousin Bunny, and all my grocery store customers. They would be disappointed if we changed our destination and I don't like disappointing anyone."

"Sadie, dear," Nathan said in a pleading tone, "how can you compare a hole in the ground to a nice hotel and a beauty school with all kinds of things you like? You'll come home looking like Marilyn Monroe."

Don looked hopeful. "You can get a Swedish massage in the school, a facial, a manicure, scalp treatments, your hair dyed and set, all different kinds of pampering for the two weeks you'll be there, all at a minimal charge. Just look at how you'll be helping Dolly, lifting her spirits, getting her out of the doldrums."

I bounced up from the armchair. "Excuse me, I'm going next door to talk to Dolly. Maybe I can convince her to go without me. Meanwhile, Nathan, give Don some schnapps. He looks like he could use a drink."

I strode to the door, opened it, and walked to the apartment at the end of the hall, glad that nobody was around to see me in my robe. I squared my shoulders and rang the bell. It took a pregnant minute before Dolly opened the door and motioned me to follow her into the well-furnished French provincial living room that didn't have plastic covers on the sofa. Dolly, her large hazel eyes, now cranberry red, was a tall, distinguished-looking woman. Tears kept rolling down her heart-shaped face over her high cheekbones and down to her silk blouse.

We sat on the pale pink sofa, my legs dangling. "Wipe your eyes, Dolly," I urged as I took some tissues from my pocket. Every piece of clothing I own has pockets for the tissues I always keep in them just in case of necessity, like now. Dolly took the tissues and dabbed at her eyes.

"Stop crying," I insisted.

Dolly stopped the stream of tears. She patted her eyes and cheeks and crumbled the tissues into a ball that she gently put in an ashtray on the marble coffee table in front of us. She kept sniffing and her look was that of utter dejection.

"Now talk to me," I ordered.

Dolly's chest heaved. "He's so good to me. He's kind and thoughtful and a good provider and I don't deserve him. I'm in no mood to take a trip and I . . . ."

"Get hold of yourself, woman. You have to go with your husband. Do you want him to turn to another woman?"

Dolly's eyes teared up again. I took out more tissues from my other pocket and handed them to her. She stopped crying and blew her nose with a trumpet sound.

"When Don went on his other business trips," I continued, "did he ask you to go along?"

Dolly nodded. "He always asked me and I always refused. I was too much in the dumps to go Brazil, France, England, Peru, Columbia, Canada, and Mexico, and all the other exotic places he went to. I can't hope for a more thoughtful, loyal, faithful husband."

Dolly sniffed and spoke in a wavering voice. "I'm such a failure."

"No, you're not. You've lost a child, the most devastating thing that could happen to a parent. But now it's time to move ahead. I feel bad for you and I want to see you get some pleasure. How about it? Will you go to Florida with Don?"

Dolly lowered her chin. "He'll leave me alone and I'll be lonesome and I just know that when Don goes selling, I'll be sitting in the hotel room looking out the window and wishing I could be back in my own home."

Thinking about the possibility of changing my travel plans, I mulled over my options. My heart went out to my depressed friend. Who knows what the woman might do if left alone? Suicide could be a way out for her and I would be responsible by not changing my mind and rescuing her. Flexibility in life is my watchword, and now I'm at a crossroads, so I agreed to change my plans.

"Will you go if Nathan and I go with you?"

Dolly's caramel-colored eyes widened. "Oh, will you? I know everything's set for your Grand Canyon tour and you were so excited about it. No. No, I can't take advantage of your good heart. I'll stay home and knit a new sweater for Don, and you go to Arizona."

"I will not," I declared. "You'll go to Florida and I'll go with you. We'll have a ball."

"Oh, you're such a good person. Kind! Considerate! Helpful! I can't thank you enough."

I felt my cheeks turn the color of borscht. I'm not used to praise. The praise I get from Nathan is when he says I do a good window display.

"But Sadie," Dolly wailed, "I don't know what clothes to take. Will you help me decide?"

"Tomorrow evening," I said as I smiled. "Right now I'm going home and flopping down on my bed. I have to get up early to open the grocery."

By the time I returned to my apartment, my husband had fallen asleep on the sofa, and Don was soused. After Don weaved his way to the door and left, I woke up Nathan by yelling, "I'll have twenty pounds of corned beef."

Nathan looked confused when he saw me sitting on my arm chair looking like I needed to speak to him. "What happened, Sadie?"

"I changed my mind because Dolly needs us to go to Florida."

"It took you long enough."

"I can be stubborn sometimes."

"Yeah, you can be, but you're always compassionate and I knew you'd come through."

That night I rolled around in my bed while Nathan snored in his. Mushrooming thoughts occupied my mind. I'll have to call the travel agent and have her cancel the Grand Canyon trip. I have to tell everyone that we changed our plans. I started feeling optimistic and I fell asleep at 3 a.m., only to hear the alarm with its shrill ring at 6 a.m. Before I got out of bed, I thought about the upcoming trip and how I would decorate the storefront display in red, white, and blue, the perfect colors for July 4th.

CHAPTER 2

The plane trip was uneventful and, when we arrived at the Gold Coast Suites, I sat next to Dolly on the elegant gray velvet sofa in the lobby while Nathan and Don checked us in at the reception desk. I always claim that I have champagne taste and a soda pocket. I know that most people call it a beer pocket, but I don't like beer. Today I burst with pleasure like Queen Elizabeth at her coronation. Perhaps Nathan was right when he objected to the Grand Canyon, the so-called big hole in the ground. I liked being a guest in a five-star hotel. A woman dripping in diamonds passed us by as she led a poodle with a diamond collar around its neck. Maybe it was rhinestones, but to me it looked like diamonds. Frankly, I can't tell the difference. I always liked diamonds and today I wore the one-half-carat diamond engagement ring Nathan gave me that I never wore in the grocery.

"This is one swanky place," I said as I examined the Art Deco coffee table in front of us.

Dolly, whose passion is interior decorating, nodded. "I like the intricate detailing of the stainless steel frame and the art nouveau styling which is further enhanced by its marble top."

"Oh, boy," I said. "You sure know a lot about decorating. As for me, I like to decorate our store window and that's it." My eyes fixed on Don. "Your husband looks great, not like he looked when he came to our door a couple of weeks ago."

"Yes, he does look like his old dapper self. And Nathan . . ."

I interrupted as I grinned. "He looks good, too, doesn't he?"

"He looks wonderful in those navy slacks and light blue golf shirt."

"I guess so," I bragged. "I shopped for new clothes for him and it does make a difference."

Dolly sighed softly. "I'm glad Don persuaded me to go to Florida."

"Are you really glad?" I looked at my friend who sat demurely with her hands folded.

"Yes, I'm feeling much better."

"So then, you'll go with me to the beauty school?"

"No, I don't feel like it," Dolly said as she watched our husbands at the reception desk.

"I'm advising you to have your hair done to lift your blue mood. I'll bet your psychiatrist would agree with me if you asked him."

Dolly frowned. "First of all, my psychiatrist, Dr. Shelly Ferguson, is a woman. Secondly, she has long gray hair she wears in a bun, and she's never stepped into a beauty parlor, let alone a beauty school. Thirdly, she has never advised me about the therapeutic value of a beauty school. In fact, since these are students, in the unlikely event of her advocating having my hair done, it wouldn't be in a beauty school where young inexperienced students make mistakes."

Dolly took a deep breath and expelled it slowly. I had never heard her deliver such a long speech. It would be hard for me to convince her to go with me to the school. I changed the topic of conversation. "How come you never went on a business trip with Don before?"

"He never insisted. And Don thought to ask you and Nathan and that makes a big difference to me. Here they come. Let's see what our rooms are like."

We watched as the tanned young bellman whisked our bags away and stacked them on a cart. We followed him to the elevator, huddling together to make room for the luggage. The elevator stopped at the fifth floor. As we emerged, my eyes fixed on an atrium that sported a flowing fountain, palm trees, and a profusion of vegetation in the center of the building with rooms surrounding it. We were shown identical suites next to each other.

Nathan tipped the porter after the young man adjusted the air-conditioner and opened the drapes to reveal a balcony that overlooked palm trees surrounding a manmade lake.

"Look," Nathan said as he pointed to a kitchenette between the living room and the bedroom. "There's a small refrigerator, a sink, and a cabinet for groceries. We can have all our meals in our room and save a bundle."

I shook my head vigorously. "I intend to eat in restaurants. Breakfast is included in the price, but this is our vacation and I'm not eating in a hotel room."

"Okay," Nathan said reluctantly as he started to unpack. "I'll put my stuff in the bottom drawer. You can have the top three drawers."

"You're so considerate." I moved over to Nathan and gave him a peck on his cheek.

"This is like a second honeymoon," Nathan said as he kissed me on my lips.

"We never really had a first honeymoon, dear. Remember when we went to a hotel in Atlantic City, I got the flu and we had to go home?"

"Yeah, I remember. It's something I can never forget. What a disappointment. We can make up for it this time."

I nodded while Nathan opened his suitcase, took out his shirts and slacks, and hung them in the closet on the kind of hangers that are fixed and no one can steal. I sat on the floral bedspread on the king-sized bed. "Dolly told me Don never insisted before that she accompany him on his business trips. I wonder why he didn't."

Nathan looked puzzled. "It's none of our business."

"Do you think he had a secret motive?"

"Don't you start your butinsky business. It don't take no amateur detective to figure out Dolly was depressed and he didn't want to stress her out."

"I guess so. He's a good husband and a great provider. You can see that Dolly is very much in love with him."

"I'm a good husband, too." Nathan pulled me down on the bed and caressed my arm.

I sighed. "I have to unpack."

"Unpack later, much, much later."

* * *

At 6 p.m., after two hours of bliss, I heard a knock at the door. "Open up folks. It's me, Don."

Nathan finger-brushed his thinning hair and opened the door. Don stood next to Dolly who wore a pretty polyester dress with a pleated skirt. She carried a purse that matched her gold sandals. "Well," Don said, "are you ready to go to dinner? There's a famous fish restaurant next to the hotel. I'm sure you'll like it."

Nathan translated in his mind 'famous' to mean expensive. "I like cafeterias," he said. "Is there one nearby?

"For dinner?" Don asked in a petulant way.

"We'll go to the fish place," I said raising my voice. "We have the reward money. Let's reward ourselves."

"It's your money, not ours," Nathan grunted.

"What's mine is yours and vice versa."

"If you insist, my lovely bride."

"I'm far from being a bride," I said as I grinned.

"You are, sweetie, as this is our first honeymoon."

"Cut the lovey dovey talk," Don said. "Let's go now as it gets crowded later. We'll mention that we're guests at this hotel and they'll give us a 10% discount."

"That's more like it," Nathan said as he steered me by my arm as we left the room.

Outside we saw a sight we had never seen in Brooklyn. A graceful swan sat on her round five-foot nest made of twigs and leaves while her mate stood alongside her. The nest made of twigs and leaves had a depression in the center.

"Wow," I said. "I have to take a picture of this." I reached into my purse and drew out my Kodak camera. I stood close to the mother swan as I clicked the button. The male raised his wings and fluffed his feathers. I took another picture. The swan moved quickly toward me. I backed away but the male was persistent in his attempt to protect his mate. My stomach muscles clenched. I began to run, and the white swan with his black feet took big steps attempting to catch me. I ran into the restaurant, breathing deeply, upset over the close call I just had with a big bird.

After we were seated, Nathan peered at the menu, pursing his lips in disgust at the high prices. I kicked him under the table, and he responded by ordering the trout, the least expensive fish. I picked the salmon, as did Dolly, and Don asked for the halibut. The older waiter shuffled over to our table with water and fresh rolls.

"It will be a half-hour before your fish is served," he said.

Nathan looked disgusted. "That long?"

"Yes, sir, all our fish is fresh and cooked to perfection."

After the waiter left, Don said, "Sorry about that swan chasing you, Sadie. All mute swans are territorial and aggressive when their mates are nesting. If he caught up with you, he could've hurt you. He weighs about twenty pounds and has a wing span about seven feet."

"Thanks for your concern," I said. "You seem to know a lot about swans."

"I always see the same two in the lake and I wanted to learn more about them so I read about mute swans. They have a black face patch and a knob on their forehead that overlays an orange bill. The male is called a cob and the female is a pen. She's probably sitting on six eggs. Swans are monogamous."

Nathan took a sip of water. "That's nice. I like it when animals eat plants."

"No, Nathan," I said. "Monogamous means they don't get divorced."

"I knew that," Nathan said. "Too many people are getting divorced. They should work out their problems, like we do."

"Actually," Don said. ". . . more than half the marriages in the U.S. end in divorce causing untold damage to the individuals, their children, and society as a whole. I think monogamy is responsible for this, not in my case, of course, but if free love was acceptable, people wouldn't have to divorce. Monogamy is forced on us by religion."

Dolly turned to her husband with a peeved expression. "What you're suggesting is unethical, immoral, and perfectly horrible."

Don squirmed in his seat. "I'm talking to pass the time, dear, just making conversation."

We continued chatting, avoiding controversial topics. The food came and that was the end of conversation.

*　　*　　*

That night I sat on the king-sized bed holding the mystery "At Betram's Hotel" by my favorite author, Agatha Christie. Last year I enjoyed reading it, and I took it along just in case I got bored and wanted to remember Jane Marple's technique for discovering murderers. I dropped off into a dreamless sleep and slept a good eight hours.

CHAPTER 3

The next morning, after breakfast on the first floor of the hotel, I set out to walk just a few yards to the beauty school, making sure to avoid my enemy, the swan. When I entered, what hit me in my generous Barbra Streisand nose was the scent of pleasant cologne, not the miserable hair spray I was used to. The gorgeous girl at the reception desk had ebony hair that flowed to her waist.

"Please sign in," the girl said politely.

"Thanks," I said as I wrote my name on a pad. There was another column for what you wanted and I wrote "wash and set."

"Here's five," I said handing Gorgeous a five-dollar bill. She gave me two dollars in change and a slip of paper and said I was to give it to the girl who would take care of me. I sat down, waited, and picked up the latest edition of *Cosmo*.

It didn't take long for a curvaceous girl, with an upturned nose and long egg-yolk-colored hair with brown roots, to call my name.

"I am Angela," she said with a heavy Hispanic accent as she shook my hand, barely grasping it. Her weak handshake was moist, her palm as soft as cream cheese.

It felt like I had shaken the leg of a chicken. I mused about the miserable shampoo this girl would attempt to give me.

She led me to a room with exquisite stations on all sides of the room. This was a beauty salon the likes of none I had ever seen. Soft music played in the background. Expensive gold and lilac-striped wallpaper lined the walls. Everything was clean and gorgeous. Shiny black wash basins were on one wall while customers draped with plastic capes sat at chairs along another wall; each station faced a mirror with ornate gold framing. Good—looking students, both male and female, wore black slacks and tops. Some were at the basins washing women's hair and one beautiful student was drying a customer's hair with a fluffy purple towel that must have cost an arm and a leg. I was surprised to see one student at a basin washing a wig. This place certainly wasn't like any beauty parlor in Brooklyn, more like a palace in a fairy land.

Angela draped a cape around my neck. She accompanied me to the sink where she proceeded to wash my hair with a lovely shampoo that smelled of lavender. I was staying in a five-star hotel and now I was in a five-star beauty school.

Sitting under the dryer with the cone-shaped metal device on my head, I put on my thinking cap. I had to come up with something new to persuade Dolly to go with me to the beauty school. She needed to get out and I didn't know where else to take her.

Nothing I had said had worked, so I had to think of something that would change her mind. I had told her she needed to get out to lift her depression. That hadn't worked. Then I told her she needed to perk up in order to keep Don interested in her. That hadn't worked. Then I tried appealing to her feminine side, about how she would look ravishing if she tried everything the beauty school offered. No go. I put my hand on my head and moved one of the curlers to scratch where it itched. The hot air shot from my hand to my brain. I had a new idea.

Dolly wasn't interested in her appearance or her mental health. She was punishing herself to bury the horrible feeling of losing her only child. But, and this was a big but, she was still functioning and was my friend. Perhaps if I told her that I needed her help to make decisions about my appearance, it might work. What color should I dye my hair? What's the best style for me? What makeup is flattering for my face, age, and body? Perhaps she would respond positively? I had to try something. If she went on the same way, it was possible that she would try suicide again and this time she could be successful. I had to save Dolly from herself.

Then a perfect idea shot through my brain. If Dolly saw what a disgusting job they did on me, she might come with me to make sure they treated me right.

Finally Angela lifted up the dryer, patted my curlers, and announced, "You done." I felt like a French fry. She tugged at the curlers and as she pulled each one, I winced.

"How long have you been in this school?"

"A few weeks I here in Miss Sophia's Beauty Academy."

"How many customers have you had?" I hoped she wouldn't say I was the first one.

"You numero uno. Don't worry. Miss Sophia taught me good."

I nodded as I bit down on my lips. The words that came to mind were not pure. But in the back of my mind I suspected I could control this so-called student.

"How you want your hair fixed?" Angela asked.

"I'm short and I want my hair teased and then sprayed so it stands up in a beehive so people will notice me and I want long bangs."

"Si, senora." Angela grabbed a round brush and began the teasing process. I looked in the mirror to see someone I didn't recognize, a witch with porcupine hair sprouting from a face with frightened blue eyes.

When she finished teasing, my eyes filled with tears but then she combed the top so high it looked like a soldier's helmet from World War I.

Then she borrowed the can of hair spray from the student in the next station and began to spray and spray and spray till a cloud of mist filled the air.

"You like?" Angela asked as she gave me a hand mirror.

"And how," I said. "It's perfect." Then I tipped her a fifty-cent coin.

She smiled as she put it in her pocket. "My first tip," she said. "Gracias."

The instructor came over to inspect the horror. "Is this how you wanted your hair styled?" she asked as she frowned. I could hardly see her through the bangs that covered my forehead and the top of my eyes.

"I like it," I said forcing a smile. "Angela follows directions perfectly."

The instructor, Miss Sophia everyone called her, shook her head. "Okay, Angela," she said in a monotone, "Good job."

Quickly I moved out the door and ran back to my room in the hotel where I found Nathan and Don who looked at me, their mouths agape.

"Don't say a word," I said. "This is just temporary."

Nathan shook his head. "It better be. Don and me are going deep-sea fishing and when we come back you better look like you."

"I will," I said, and like an arrow I ran to Dolly's room. I banged on the door.

When Dolly opened the door, she looked at me and gasped. "My God, what did you do to yourself?"

I felt my cheeks redden with embarrassment. "What do you mean?" I asked.

"You look completely different."

"I had a wash and set at the beauty school."

"You look like . . . . There are no words for what you look like."

"I look fabulous, don't I?"

Dolly waited a few moments to compose herself. "Fabulous? You look horrible. You're a pretty woman but now you look like Frankenstein's wife."

"But, Dolly, the beehive is the most popular style for 1966."

Dolly collapsed in an armchair. "But not for you. You're too short. It makes you look like you have a huge head on a small body, like an alien. And how can you see with those bangs over your eyes?"

"I can see between the hairs."

"You go right back there and demand they give you an advanced student, one who knows what she's doing."

I shook my head. "I can't do that. I told the instructor that I liked the style."

"It makes no difference what you said. Tell them you changed your mind. A woman is allowed to change her mind. Tell them you couldn't see because the bangs hung over your eyes and when you went back to the hotel, you pushed the bangs up, looked in the mirror and screamed."

"I'm too embarrassed to say that."

"Then tell them that when your husband looked at you he said he wanted a divorce."

"I can't lie. I was never good at lying. When my cousin Bunny asks if I notice she lost five pounds, and she looks the same, I say that she looks wonderful but I can't tell her she's thinner." *It isn't true that I'm not good at lying. Actually telling a believable lie is one of my attributes.*

"What can I say to change your mind?"

"You can say you'll go and tell them you want me to have an advanced student and a new flattering hairstyle."

"All right, Sadie. I'll go back there with you and order them to undo the mess free of charge."

I nodded with my head down as I didn't want Dolly to see me grinning. I had won. Dolly was finally going to go out in the world. My suffering had paid off.

*　　*　　*

When we entered the beauty school, Dolly approached the receptionist, and demanded to see the owner. A minute later, Miss Sophia glided into the front room. I hadn't known that, not only was she the instructor, but she also owned the palatial beauty school. Miss Sophia, who looked like she was in her thirties, was built like a model dressed in a form-fitting lilac uniform. Diamond earrings, the size of raisins, adorned her earlobes.

"May I speak with you?" Dolly asked calmly.

"Of course," Miss Sophia answered.

"My name is Dolly Morris and this is Sadie Weinstein."

Dolly took my arm and swung me in front of Miss Sophia. "This is my neighbor and dear friend and she had her hair done less than an hour ago. Tell the God's honest truth, what do you think of this hairdo?"

Miss Sophia scrutinized my head. She spoke with a clipped British accent that sounded like it was put on. "It's not my taste but your friend asked for this style. If she changed her mind, I'll be happy to assign her to another student who will change the style. There will be no charge. And if you want, you can also have your hair done by another more experienced student, also free of charge. Please accept my apologies to you both."

"That's more like it," Dolly said.

I was thrilled. Now Dolly was hooked into using the beauty school which I had planned all along.

Dolly said, "I just want my hair washed and set, not cut."

Miss Sophia nodded. "Of course. But ladies, regrettably, I require your patience for just a short time while I give my new students a lesson in head washing."

I piped up, "We'll watch. Maybe we'll learn how to wash our own heads correctly."

Miss Sophia clapped her hands. "Attention everyone! Most of the students with clients continue with what you're doing. I want the following students to report to the end sink."

Glancing around the room, in her strict teacher's voice, she called out, "Angela and Ricardo."

I peered at Ricardo and saw a confident, handsome young man.

Angela swaggered over and stood on the right side of the sink. I took a spot on the left side next to Dolly, so I could carefully observe how to wash someone's hair.

Angela announced with a sneer, "I no need lesson again."

Standing with her hands on her hips, Miss Sophia said, "It won't hurt you to repeat it since you didn't learn it right the first time."

Angela tossed her head defiantly. She hooked a hank of her hair behind her ear, from which a beaded earring hung. "Bueno shampoo I give woman. I know how."

By this time Miss Sophia had enough lip. "If you don't want me to expel you and send your sorry butt back to Columbia, you will repeat this lesson until you get it right."

Angela kept quiet, her eyes betraying her anger as she stared defiantly at Miss Sophia.

"I'm annoyed with this delay," Dolly proclaimed.

"Would you like to be the subject and have your hair washed right now?" Miss Sophia asked Dolly in a more polite tone than she used talking to the students.

Dolly squinted at the sink with the cushioned chair in front. "If this will take a short time, okay."

Miss Sophia pointed to Angela who stood scratching her head. "Angela, show us how you would begin with this client."

I watched Angela take Dolly by the arm, steer her to the shampoo chair, and push her down.

Dolly shouted, "Unhand me, girl."

The muscles in Miss Sophia's face tightened. "Don't ever lay a hand on a client to seat her." She waited a moment. "You show your client to the shampoo chair and help her become comfortable. Repeat the procedure."

What a tough cookie Miss Sophia is, I thought. But I guess she's just doing her job.

Dolly exclaimed in a high pitched voice, "I'm not getting up. Let's get on with it."

Miss Sophia bobbed her head to acknowledge Dolly's strong objection. "All right, Angela, what do you do next?"

Grabbing a plastic robe, Angela began to drape it around Dolly's neck.

Miss Sophia raised her voice. "No, that's all wrong. Ricardo, you demonstrate the next step."

Ricardo took a purple fluffy terry cloth towel from a drawer and moved to the left side of the chair. Carefully he turned the collar of Dolly's blouse to the inside. Then he folded the towel lengthwise and diagonally across Dolly's shoulders, and crossed the ends under her chin. He placed the shampoo cape over the towel, and fastened it in the back.

Miss Sophia, next to Ricardo, bent over to examine the back of Dolly's neck. "You did the right thing when you made sure that the cape didn't touch the client's skin. What comes next?"

"I'm not sure," Ricardo said as he shook his head.

"You place a second towel over the cape and secure it to the front," Miss Sophia demonstrated the procedure.

"Listen and learn," Miss Sophia ordered. "If the client has glasses and/or jewelry, you politely ask her to remove them. Hand her purse to her and make sure she puts those items away. What's next?"

Ricardo raised his hand. In a strong masculine voice he said, "I read about it. I know it all. You look at a woman's scalp to see if she has sores. After the examination you rest the client's head in the bowl." He smiled confidently like a cat with a sardine.

"Very good. You examine the scalp to be sure there are no abrasions. If there are, you call me over. Then what?"

"You turn on the faucet, let the water run until there is a good temperature."

"Nice," Miss Sophia said. "This is important. You must adjust the volume and temperature."

Miss Sophia continued, "You test the water temperature on your inner wrist and monitor it by keeping your fingers under the spray. Remember to ask the client if she's comfortable with the temperature of the water. Next you saturate the hair with the water, lifting the hair, and with a free hand work it, all the time protecting the client's face, ears, and neck from spray."

Oh boy, I thought, Angela did everything wrong.

Dolly, who had been sitting upright in the chair, started to sneeze. Miss Sophia motioned to Angela to get some tissues. Angela grabbed a couple from the shelf, moved to Dolly's left side pushing me roughly, and handed her the tissues.

Without warning, Dolly's face turned bright red. She screamed, "Sadie!" as she toppled from the chair to the floor, her body convulsing as she thrashed, her features twisting into a grotesque mask; then abruptly she stopped moving.

My heart pounded as I bent down to encircle her inert body, noticing a puncture wound on her neck near her hairline with a pinprick of blood around it. I felt for a pulse in her wrist. There was none. I tried breathing into her mouth. She didn't stir.

I wailed! "It's my fault. Please live, Dolly. Please come back. Please." A knot tightened in my throat. I felt the first prick of tears in my eyes.

Everyone in the room stopped short. Fear in the room spread like acne on a teenager's face. A student, who was doing a touchup with a brush on a woman's hair, splashed the dye on her face. A girl styling a mannequin's wig dropped it. Miss Sophia raced to her office as she yelled, "I'll call 911."

The keening sounds of my grief wiped out the sirens of the ambulance and the squad car that responded to the emergency call. I was frantic. I lost track of the time it took the ambulance to come. I held Dolly's lifeless body in my arms, as my tears soaked her clothes.

Meanwhile, Miss Sophia ordered every student to the other side of the room away from Dolly. When the officer bent down and pulled me to my feet, I collapsed in his arms. I felt like my life's blood had been drained from me. The officer placed me in a cushioned chair in front of another sink. I held on tight to the armrests.

I watched as an emergency medical team began their examination. When an EMT found no heartbeat, he used the defibrillator. He compressed Dolly's chest with machine-like precision. Another EMT injected her with a needle. A tube was put down her throat. "The monitor is flat lined," the pimply-faced emergency medical technician stated in no uncertain terms.

I let out a piercing scream. "No, no," I cried. *She'd be alive if I hadn't encouraged her to come here.*

"Did she have heart trouble?" the officer asked me.

Tears rolled down my face. "She was my friend. I would know if she had heart trouble. She didn't. She turned red, had a convulsion, and collapsed."

"Did she have epilepsy?" the officer asked.

"No." I didn't have the strength to wipe the mucus that dripped from my nose.

"She was murdered," I whispered. "I think someone who was near her injected her with poison. Didn't you see the puncture on her neck near her hairline? I don't know who did it or why, but I'll find out if it's the last thing I do." I wiped the tears from my face with my hand.

"Joe," the officer said to his buddy, "contact Sheriff Neely, Detective Lenhart and his partner, Detective Gaspard, the medical examiner, the photographer, and the rest of the forensic team."

He turned to the students and the women in the beauty chairs. "Everyone will wait in this room until the Sheriff arrives."

The students and clients spoke noisily, some shook their heads with concern, and others looked sad and distraught. I heard loud sighs in the room.

Feeling faint, I leaned over and put my head between my knees. I was living a nightmare.

It didn't take long before two detectives arrived, a tall man and a short woman. The woman just stood quietly and looked down at Dolly. The man was tall with dark curly hair. He moved over to the lead paramedic and spoke to him. I moved close to them and eavesdropped.

"I'm Detective Lenny Lenhart," he said in a low voice.

My hearing is keen and I heard everything. I shifted into my amateur detective mode.

"Yeah, detective, what's up?" the paramedic asked.

"Fill me in," Detective Lenhart said.

"The down time was 10:30 according to the instructor, Miss Sophia, who called us a minute later. Police on the scene at 10:38. We arrived 10:45. Multiple shocks. Intubated with good air movement. Full drug resuscitation and good compressions. Monitor was flatlined. We got nothing. Puncture wound on left side of neck near hairline. The defibrillator monitor's screen showed a single green horizontal line. Between you and the ME's review, I imagine the standard procedure for a death of indeterminate cause will be an autopsy."

"Gotchya. I agree."

Ricardo, Angela, Miss Sophia, and I were taken to the police station. The rest of the students and clients in the beauty school were dismissed. I assumed that the police wanted to question just the people who had surrounded Dolly. We sat squirming on hard metal chairs in the detective's boxlike office. The detective had a tough bearing and looked at us questioningly with world-weary eyes.

"Does anyone here know anything about Dolly Morris's death?" he asked in a crisp, straightforward way.

Slowly I raised my hand. "I think something was injected into her neck that caused her death."

"For now, let's presume Dolly Morris was murdered. I will question the four of you in turn. Meanwhile, you will sit in the outer office. I'll start with you." The detective pointed to Miss Sophia. We were escorted by a cop to a large office with gray walls, and seated at separate desks.

An officer with an unpleasant garlic breath questioned me. He asked my name, permanent and temporary address, date of birth, arrest record. I took a breath of stale air that smelled of old donuts and cigarette smoke.

CHAPTER 4

"In your own words, please tell me what happened." Detective Lenhart spoke soothingly to Miss Sophia.

"I'm the owner and head instructor in Miss Sophia's Beauty Academy. I've been there for three years and we never had anyone die before today. It's very upsetting." Miss Sophia wiped drops of perspiration from her upper lip.

"I know this is hard for you, but please go on."

"Well, this Sadie Weinstein had her hair done earlier today by Angela Lopez, and she came back with her friend, Dolly Morris. They didn't like the job Angela did. It was really atrocious, so I said they could have it done over, and I wouldn't charge either of them. Anyway, before we went ahead I had to give a head washing lesson. Ricardo, Angela, and Sadie Weinstein were gathered around the sink and I was in the middle. Dolly Morris was sitting on the chair. Ricardo was ready to wash her hair. I don't know what happened exactly, but I clearly remember that Dolly's face turned beet red, and she screamed, 'Sadie,' as she went into a convulsion. I assume that Sadie had somehow murdered her and she identified the murderer. Then, when she stopped thrashing, Sadie Weinstein bent down to examine her and she yelled, 'It's my fault.' I never would have taken her for a killer. I went to my office and called 911 and that's all I know."

*   *   *

With tears stinging my eyes, I sat uncomfortably at Detective Lenhart's desk. His female partner wasn't present. Dolly was dead and it was my fault.

"Right now, we don't know if Mrs. Morris was murdered but an autopsy will determine the cause of death and, if it is murder, you are a suspect," the detective said, his voice low, his accent Southern.

I gasped. How could that be? "Why?"

"There is a wound on her neck and you were standing close to her."

"So were Ricardo, and Angela, and don't leave out Miss Sophia. Dolly was my friend. I didn't kill her. I never killed anyone." I took a deep breath to smother my frustration and anger at this unjust accusation.

The detective tapped his pen on his desk with such force that it made me even more nervous.

"Mrs. Dolly Morris was heard to scream your name before she had a convulsion. Many victims name their killers right before they die." Detective Lenhart shot me a piercing look.

That he thought I could be guilty of an unproven murder sent a jolt of pain through me. A part of my brain fizzled. "Dolly called out to me to help her. You know when you're in heavy labor you call for your mother."

"Mrs. Weinstein, I never gave birth and I never called for my mother even when I was shot. I don't know the motivation for the possible murder, but you're the only person acquainted with Dolly Morris."

"I'll help you find the motivation and the murderer. I've worked with the police in Brooklyn when it took months before the killer was caught. I was instrumental in finding him. In fact, they gave me the award money and I used part of it to come here."

"I'd prefer if you did not help us. In fact, I don't want you doing any investigating. Why did you say it was your fault Mrs. Morris died? Don't deny this as you were overheard by witnesses."

"I persuaded her to go to Florida even though she was dead set against going." *Oh boy, every time I open my mouth I put my foot in it. Why did I say dead set? Oy vey!*

Detective Lenhart's dark brown eyes widened. "Why didn't she want to go and why did you want her to?"

"Dolly was depressed over the loss of her only child. Her husband came to our apartment and said that her psychiatrist thought a change of environment would do her good. At first, I didn't want to change our plans about going to the Grand Canyon, but when I saw how depressed Dolly really was, I told her that my husband and I would go and she changed her mind."

The detective fiddled with his pen. "Why did you take her to the beauty academy?"

"After a woman gets fixed up, she feels better, and I thought it would be better for her than to remain in the hotel room with only the TV for company."

"But why a beauty academy and not a beauty salon?"

"Her husband does business there and it's in walking distance of the hotel."

The detective nodded. "I see."

"May I go now?" I asked.

"Yes, Mrs. Weinstein, but don't leave Miami Beach. Now I have to tell Mr. Morris about his wife."

"But he and my husband went deep sea fishing and they won't be back till this evening," I said as I wrung my hands.

* * *

The night air was heavy with moisture and the temperature hadn't dropped more than two degrees. Florida in the summer was hot as Hades. Lenhart and Gaspard waited in the air-conditioned car until they observed two men, each carrying a fishing rod and tackle box, enter the hotel.

"Let's go, Julie," Lenhart said.

"Not yet. Let's give them ten minutes to return to their rooms." Julie took a piece of gum from a package and chewed with the intensity of a waterfall.

The detectives approached the door of Don's room. Lenny knocked.

The door opened and Don Morris stood there in his bathrobe.

"We're from Homicide and we'd like to talk with you. I'm Detective Lenhart and this is Detective Gaspard." Lenhart and Gaspard held out their badges for Don to inspect.

"I can't imagine what you want with me?" Don said.

"Please let us in and we'll tell you," Lenhart said in a soothing voice.

"Come in then. I'll turn off the TV. Take a seat and get to the point. Is it bad news?"

"I'll tell you what happened," Gaspard said. "Yes, it's bad news."

"Spit it out." Don's eyes were wary.

Gaspard took out her chewing gum and put it in a tissue. "Your wife was about to have her hair washed in the beauty academy. They were demonstrating how to give a proper shampoo and . . . ."

"That doesn't sound like my wife. She said she wouldn't go to the beauty school."

"It seems that Sadie Weinstein persuaded her and there is no doubt that it was your wife, Dolly."

"So what happened?"

"She collapsed and died."

"I don't believe you. Why would she die? She was a healthy person, only a little depressed."

"Maybe she committed suicide," Gaspard volunteered.

"While having her head washed? Impossible."

"So, what really happened?"

Lenhart cleared his throat. "There was a puncture on her neck. Maybe someone injected her with poison. We'd like you to give us permission to do an autopsy."

Don's face turned red as a radish. "My God, I can't believe this." He shook his head vigorously.

We knocked loudly at the door. Lenhart opened it. Nathan and I strode in.

I was still looking ridiculous with my hairdo but I hadn't had a chance to do anything about it. "I'm so sorry, Don," I said.

"I'm sorry, too," Nathan said as he put his hand on Don's shoulder. Don hung his head and wiped a few tears from his eyes.

"I'm sorry, sir," Lenhart said. "The coroner will have to do an autopsy to determine the cause of death."

"Don't allow it, Don," I cried. "It's against our religion."

"I want to know what killed my wife," Don said in a low voice. "You may do the autopsy."

"You're making a big mistake," I said.

"Mrs. Weinstein," Lenhart said. "Keep out of this. In this case, we don't need the husband's permission. By law we have to do an autopsy when the cause of death is undetermined. Is it possible you don't want the police to discover it was murder, and you're the murderer?"

My eyes burned with anger. *The nerve of him to accuse me.*

Lenhart continued, "If this is a murder, Mr. Morris, don't you want to know who did it and bring the person to justice?"

"Yes, of course."

I collapsed in an armchair. *Why did I have to persuade Dolly to go to the beauty school? When will I learn to mind my own business?*

CHAPTER 5

Detective Lenhart and Detective Gaspard stopped at a donut shop on their way to get the results of the autopsy. Julie had a muffin and coffee. Lenny polished off two chocolate covered donuts. The total came to four donuts for the day and the day was only half over. He was divorced and used donuts as a pick-me-up. Not caring that his belly hung two inches over his pants, he indulged himself freely. Whenever he went to that place that had the sickening smell of formaldehyde, and dead bodies cut wide open, he wished he could be at the beach, any place but there.

As he drove to the medical examiner's building, he thought about that bag of wind, Dr. Lucius Porter, who bragged about how he was the best forensic pathologist in the business. Porter used jargon like arrows flying through the air. Most of the gibberish was so technical, he couldn't understand it. The man was the most pompous individual with whom he had the misfortune to deal. Now parking in front of the building that looked like a cement coffin, his stomach ached and he realized he shouldn't have eaten those doughy donuts. Julie was quiet, for once not chewing gum.

The large room was drab, uncarpeted, and cold. Lenhart shivered as he approached the braggart who luckily wasn't cutting up anyone at the time. The detective tended to puke when he saw blood and intestines hanging out. The jerk, his opinion of him, sat at his metal desk pouring over some paperwork. He didn't look like what he thought a medical examiner should look like, a tall brawny guy with popping muscles. Instead, this fellow was thin, and as short as a jockey. He sported bifocals so thick that the detective wondered how he could see. He wore a red flannel, long-sleeved shirt with a bolo that had a scorpion embedded in a clear plastic oval.

"Hi, Doc," Lenhart said. "Do you have the report on Dolly Morris?"

"Affirmative. The lethal injection on the left side of her neck near her hairline came from the poison-dart frog."

"So she was murdered," Julie said.

"A frog? A little frog?" Lenhart mused.

"Not just any frog. I said the poison-dart frog." Porter gave him a sour smile.

"Where does this frog live? Could it come from Columbia?" When he had questioned Angela and Ricardo, they had said they came from Columbia.

The doctor's voice dripped like sugar laced with strychnine. "There are five species of poison-dart frogs known as Dendrobates. The frog is an amphibian, usually they're small, about 1 to 2 ½ inches and weigh about two grams. They're brightly colored, gorgeous in fact. They come in a stunning cobalt blue and some beauties are cadmium yellow and ebony black. They're diurnal."

"What the hell does that mean?"

"It means they're up during the day."

"So why the hell didn't you say that?"

"You're a college graduate. Don't you know what nocturnal and diurnal mean?"

"Didn't you hear me? I don't give a damn about the frog. Where does it come from?"

"Don't get your bowels in an uproar, detective. These frogs are endemic to the humid, tropical environments of Central and South America. It could come from Columbia."

"This is Miami Beach. We live in a tropical environment. Could it come from here?"

"No poison-dart frogs have been found in Florida. The Amerindians use the frogs' toxic secretions to poison the tips of blow darts."

The detective bit down on his lips. This guy was getting on his nerves worse than when his wife used to wake him in the middle of the night to tell him she couldn't sleep. "Tell me how the poison works."

"It's not poison per se. It's really a venom called batrachotoxin and it causes rapid death by acting on the muscles and the nervous system and paralyzing in seconds. It's usually delivered directly into the lymphatic system where it acts faster. This gal was pierced with a needle and then the needle was probably put into some small tube and hidden."

"How did the perp get hold of the stuff and get it to Florida?"

"That's your job to find out. My job is to determine the cause of death and that's just what I did and speedily. I happen to be acquainted with this venom and I ran the tests for it. Another doctor would have taken weeks to come up with the same results. You owe me one. It's going to be an arduous job for you to catch the culprit."

"You did your job and I'll do mine. You can rest assured I'll get that perp."

Lenhart moved toward the door. He turned to his partner. "Let's get the hell out of here."

*   *   *

Nathan and I sat on the sofa in the living room of our suite. We watched the news on TV in an effort to calm down from the terrible reality of Dolly's death.

In his crisp voice, the news anchor announced, "The latest on Vietnam. Fighting continues by the Marine Corps in its effort to eliminate North Vietnamese Army forces from the DMZ."

I tried to make conversation that had nothing to do with Dolly. "What's the DMZ?"

Nathan stared at me. "It's the Demilitarized Zone. How come you don't know this?"

"How should I know? I'm in the grocery business in Brooklyn and we don't have demilitarized zones. If it's demilitarized, why are they fighting there?"

"It's a riddle, Sadie. Anyway, I'm getting hungry. You didn't eat lunch. Ain't you hungry?"

I listened to my stomach rumble. "I'd like to go to that fancy fish restaurant next door," I said hopefully.

"You bet, my sweetie. You've been under a lot of stress and you deserve a good meal out."

"I love you, Nathan."

"I know."

CHAPTER 6

It was another sunny morning when Nathan, in his pajamas, opened his door to pick up the newspaper and saw Don in the corridor. "How are you feeling? What's up?"

Don, dressed in gabardine slacks and a short-sleeved shirt, had shaved and showered. "I had a call from Detective Lenhart. Dolly was murdered. They're releasing her body and I have to make burial arrangements."

"I'm sorry." Nathan's head drooped. "If you wait a few minutes, I'll wash and dress and go with you."

"I can go myself. The Sinai Funeral Home is close by."

Nathan shook his head. "It ain't something to do alone. Wait in your room and I'll be there in a jiffy."

"If you insist."

"I do insist. How are you feeling, Don?

"I'm bearing up under the strain. Actually, I'm just in a state of shock."

When Nathan stepped back and closed the door he saw me still in bed. He asked, "Are you sleeping?"

I opened one eye. "Not anymore."

"Don just told me it's confirmed, Dolly was murdered. He's going to the funeral home and I'm going with him."

"Oy vey! I knew it. Who would murder a kind woman like Dolly? Now I'm suspect number one."

Nathan pulled on a pair of shorts. "Let the police handle this one. Keep out of it."

"I will," I said, thinking otherwise.

"What will you do when I'm gone?"

"I'll go to the beauty academy and have my hair styled."

"Just make sure you don't act like a detective and chase down clues."

*   *   *

I had to learn about the poison that killed Dolly, but I knew Detective Lenhart, the blockhead, and Detective Gaspard, the gum chewer, wouldn't reveal the information. If I was to proceed with my investigation, and I certainly would, there had to be another way. I wouldn't put up with the stench of failure.

I stood on the balcony, my eyes surveying my enemy, the swan in the lake, frustrated by a solution that wasn't forthcoming. The steamy air in Miami Beach was oppressive and I wiped the perspiration that collected on my upper lip. As this wasn't a good place to think, I opened the glass sliding door and stepped inside my wonderfully air-conditioned hotel room. Instead of making myself comfortable on the soft armchair that would prompt me to snooze, I chose to sit on the chair next to the desk piled high with attractive Florida entertainment brochures.

Noticing the empty envelope on the desk with the maid's name, Juanita, it reminded me we would have to leave her a hefty tip when we left for home. Until Dolly's murder was solved, the detectives wouldn't dismiss their primary suspect, ME.

I moved over to the tiny kitchenette opposite the bathroom. In the refrigerator were two bottles of water, a jar of peanut butter, orange marmalade, a loaf of pumpernickel, and eight vanilla yogurts. I had no appetite. I needed something strong like coffee, and happily the hotel provided a coffee machine, two white china cups, and packets of coffee, sugar, and powdered creamer.

After the coffee perked, I sat down with my cup, sipped the hot, refreshing liquid slowly, and tried to coax my mushy brain cells into a plan for learning more about what killed Dolly. Sometimes I prefer cleaning my oven to thinking, which is tough. I hummed a song that was often played on the radio and sung by Dusty Springfield, *You Don't Have To Say You Love Me*. It was a popular song for 1966. I was hooked by the melody and Nathan told me over and over that he was getting fed up with hearing me hum the same song. I paid him no attention. What I hummed was my business.

By the time I finished my coffee, I came up with a terrific idea. First, I would have to find out where the morgue was located, and then I would go there, wait around until someone came out and talk to that person. Somehow I would elicit the information I needed to pursue the criminal. In my heart, I knew that, if I wasn't a lady with a grocery in Brooklyn, I would be a private eye. I kept reading every book that Agatha Christie wrote and I took out books from the library about crime and how to catch a criminal. My great-grandmother in Lithuania had solved the mystery of who killed the butcher's wife. This was in my blood and there was no denying my calling.

CHAPTER 7

After I finished my coffee and showered, I dressed in my sexiest clothes, my lilac dress with ruffles on the hem which were two inches above my knees. I slipped on my stiletto heels, removed my wedding ring and put it in my purse. Since I hadn't yet been in the sun, there was no white telltale mark. So all in all, I looked my best and hoped I could make an impression on any man who worked in the morgue.

Downstairs I bought two chocolate bars in the gift shop and walked the few yards to the beauty academy where I had my hair washed and set by Joel, a handsome young man who was an advanced student. I asked for a page boy and he did a good job. Angela glared at me.

"Joel," I said. "Do you happen to know where the morgue is located?"

"No, Mrs. Weinstein, but I'll look in the phone book."

He provided me with the address. I went back to my hotel room and left a note for Nathan telling him I'd be away for a while. Nathan had already gone with Don to the funeral home and he wouldn't miss me.

I took the elevator to the lobby and asked the concierge to hail a taxi for me.

The tall man with a hooked nose and small eyes, smiled. "Of course, madam. Taking a sightseeing tour of Miami Beach, are you?"

"Yes," I said, thinking that this poor fellow would step out of his skin if he knew I was going to the morgue.

I gave the taxi driver the address of the morgue. We drove there in silence and stopped at a small, gray building and I placed myself near the front door. It was getting close to lunch time and I hoped people would be leaving to go to luncheonettes for sustenance. I waited fifteen minutes and was halfway through the first candy bar when an obese, young woman stepped out. She wore an orange cotton dress and looked like a Halloween pumpkin. Quickly she strutted down the block and was on the verge of opening the door of a Buick Skylark when I caught up with her.

"Miss, please may I speak with you for a moment?" I asked as politely as I could.

"You may not," she said brashly as she entered the car and drove off.

Disgusted, I moved back to the same spot in front of the morgue and waited ten minutes before a man came out. He looked kind of strange. I thought he was the janitor, a pencil-thin, short man like me, and I'm really petite. This guy wore thick bifocals and, even though one could fry an egg on the sidewalk under the topical sun, he wore a red flannel, long-sleeved shirt. I hate scorpions but this fellow had a scorpion in a bolo around his freckled neck. I stopped him.

"Excuse me, sir. May I talk to you for a minute?"

"What do you want? I gave to the Red Cross already today."

I drew in my breath. "Oh no, sir, I'm not soliciting, money or anything else. I just saw you emerge from the morgue and I assume you work there."

"So?"

"Well, you see I'm writing a murder mystery and it involves the victim having an autopsy in a morgue. I would appreciate if you could describe a morgue, and maybe a little about an autopsy."

"Very interesting. How about we go to the diner around the corner, have a bite of lunch, and I'll tell you what a morgue looks like?"

The small man peered at me through his thick glasses. I noticed he wasn't wearing a wedding ring. I was somewhat apprehensive about dining with a man other than Nathan, but I had to investigate thoroughly, didn't I?

"That's very kind of you."

"I like to talk to a pretty woman any time."

Biting down on my lips, I wondered who this guy really was. We strolled around the corner and took a booth in the back of the diner. I picked up the menu and studied it. Could I let a strange man feed me? Was it the right thing to do? Would Nathan be jealous if he ever found out? I could and I would. "I'll have a tuna fish sandwich, French fries, and a Coke, please."

"Good choice," the man said. "I'll have the same."

We ate in silence, but I lingered over my soda, waiting for him to finish so I could question him.

When he took the bite of the last fry, I opened up. "My name is Sheila Weinberg and I have ten chapters already completed for my mystery novel *Road to Hell*. I really appreciate what you're doing."

"Think nothing of it. I read mysteries and usually by the second chapter I know who the murderer is. I was top in my class at Harvard. I'm the chief medical examiner and there is no one more knowledgeable in the whole U.S.A. than me."

Oh my, oh my. This guy is not the janitor but a gasbag, a certifiable peacock who preens. "I told you my name but you haven't told me yours."

"I'm Dr. Lucas Porter. When the prosecuting attorney wants an expert witness, they call me and they're never disappointed."

"Really?"

"Why would I lie?"

"I'm sorry. I didn't mean to imply that you're lying."

"That's okay. Just ask me anything about my work. I like to talk about it. I take great pride in being the best medical examiner around."

"What does a morgue look like?"

"There are no windows and it's air-conditioned like the Artic. That's why I wear a flannel shirt. I'm used to the smell which bothers some people but not me. It's Chanel #5 to me. Contrary to what most people think, there is no blood on the cement floors or walls. I like to work in a clean environment. Of course, we have all kinds of equipment for cutting up the bodies, like saws and such. Wouldn't you like to know more about the process?"

I sipped my soda. "Yeah, sure. Please tell me about a recent interesting case."

Dr. Porter grinned. "I just had an unusual one. A dame, I mean a woman, was brought in with a bloody mark on her neck. I was told that she was on a chair with her neck exposed, when she had a convulsion, and died almost immediately. I found no direct brain pathology so I immediately suspected a neurotoxin. I isolated the venom of the Columbian poison-dart frog. A damn fine pick-up, if I say so myself."

"Well, I'm so impressed with your thoroughness. Did you learn anything else?"

Dr. Porter smirked. "Four people who stood near her are suspects in this woman's death."

"That is a most unusual case. Where do these poison-dart frogs live?"

"Most of them are found in Columbia. They're pretty little animals, almost as pretty as you."

I knew it. It was Angela for sure. I remembered when Miss Sophia had said she'd send her sorry butt back to Columbia. It wouldn't be hard for her to obtain the stuff, but it was time for me to get away from this egocentric bag of wind.

"Thank you for the information and for the food." I rose from my seat.

"Will I see you again?" he asked as he reached for the check.

"You never know when we'll meet again."

"How about dinner tomorrow night? I'll pick you up and take you to a high class restaurant. A lady like you deserves the best."

I felt like disappearing like vanishing cold cream. My jaw tightened. Thinking fast, I said, "Tomorrow I'll be going to Georgia to my cousin's son's bar-mitzvah. Why don't you give me your number and I'll call you when I get back."

He looked disappointed but carefully gave me his card. I put it in my purse. I may have to see him again. This is all part of my career as an amateur detective. I had an idea that the murderer would show up at Dolly's funeral and planned to go with Nathan.

CHAPTER 8

At 9 a.m. the day of the funeral, Nathan and I knocked at Don's door. When he opened the door I noticed that he was dressed, and shaved, and the complimentary newspaper that was left in front of the door had already been taken in by him. I was shocked that he wore Bermuda shorts and a t-shirt. But I guess to each his own.

"How are you holding up?" I asked.

"Not good. I feel like a truck ran over me. Dolly and I were married fifteen years and now I'm all alone and despondent."

We took the elevator to the parking garage and Don sat in back of the rented car. Nathan drove on the MacArthur Causeway, the bridge over Biscayne Bay that connected Miami Beach with Miami. I looked out the passenger seat window at the cruise ships that lined the nearby Port of Miami and felt terrible that Dolly would never admire the fluffy clouds in the bright blue sky, or smell the sweet scent of roses. The Causeway was over three miles, and as we neared Miami, I saw the building that housed the *Miami Herald*. The story of Dolly's murder had been front page news, and Don had refused to have her obituary in the paper saying that he wanted no strangers at the funeral.

We stopped in front of the chapel at Beth David Memorial Gardens and went in. At least we would have the service in the comfort of an air-conditioned room. To my surprise we were the only people there. A young woman handed us a booklet which was written in Hebrew and English, the prayer for the dead, the Kaddish, and the 23rd psalm in English. A medium-sized Rabbi entered. He spoke quietly to Don who moved over to us when the Rabbi left the room. Don talked to me in low tones. "I didn't want to bother aunts, uncles and cousins by asking them to Dolly's funeral. They'd have to fly in and they can't afford it."

"That's considerate of you," I said.

Don added, "I just told the Rabbi a few things about Dolly's life."

When the Rabbi stepped out of the chapel, I poked Nathan in the ribs, "I want to speak to you in private." I got up and Nathan followed me to the lobby.

I jerked my thumb toward a window that showed hundreds of graves throughout the cemetery. "Nathan, just look and see how many pink azalea bushes there are around, green bushes too. I think they're called boxwood bushes."

Nathan lifted his black yarmulke and scratched his head. "So?"

"So, when we go to the gravesite, I want you to look behind the bushes for the killer."

"I don't think I can do that."

"Why not?"

"I'll look like a fool."

"Who cares? You look behind the bushes and I'll look behind any palm trees that are nearby. It's vital we find the killer."

"The Rabbi is going into the chapel. Let's get back to our seats, Sadie." He took my hand and led me to the front of the chapel. I hoped he'd do as I directed.

The Rabbi cleared his throat and spoke clearly in a cultured manner.

"We are here to honor the brief life of a woman who was a good person. She was active in the Hadassah, had studied interior design, and loved animals. Dolly Morris left us without a goodbye, with a violent death. I didn't have the opportunity to meet Dolly when she was alive, but her husband has only the highest praise for her. Don, I am deeply sorry for your loss. You will grieve in your own way. Grief is the price we pay for love. Now Dolly has gone to her final resting place where there is peace."

Later the Rabbi led us to an open grave where a plain pine casket was suspended. The cemetery looked like one of the most beautiful areas I had ever seen. There was a small bridge over a brook that looked like the one in the Japanese garden in Botanic Garden in Brooklyn. Tall stately palm trees circled the cemetery.

I moved to the thick palm tree closest to the grave. The killer wasn't there. I hurried back and whispered to Nathan. "Go quietly now and look behind those bushes."

Nathan walked away and came back quickly. "I ain't seen no one."

I held the umbrella over my head when the Rabbi spoke, "Let us say the 23rd Psalm."

I opened the booklet and couldn't stop the flow of tears but without seeing the words I said the 23rd Psalm by heart. I took tissues out of the pocket of my dress, and wiped my tears and the perspiration that had collected on my forehead.

Suddenly people collected at the gravesite. I shuddered to see Miss Sophia, Angela, and Ricardo. *What were they doing here?* Angela was twining her hair around her finger, and Ricardo stood like a statue. They were dressed in the outfits they wore at the beauty school.

Miss Sophia blurted out, "I brought my students who were gathered next to Dolly Morris when she died. I thought it the proper step to take. We are all sorry for her painful death. May she rest in peace."

Don looked at Miss Sophia when she spoke. He looked surprised but didn't shed a tear.

The casket was lowered and Don and everyone present scooped a mound of earth and tossed it on Dolly's grave. I was shocked that Miss Sophia had brought the students who had been near Dolly right before she was murdered. If only Angela had shown up, then it would've confirmed my suspicion that she was the killer. Now I would have to dig deeper.

As we left the cemetery, I saw Detective Lenhart and his partner in a car watching everyone. He had the same idea as I that the murderer would be present at the funeral, but it didn't happen that way.

When we came to the hotel, Don went to his room and we went to ours.

Nathan took off his long pants and put on shorts and I removed my dress. I put on a cotton summer dress, and sat down on the sofa in the living room to relax from the ordeal of the funeral.

"Nathan, I noticed that Don didn't cry. He looked sad but he didn't cry at the funeral."

"Some men ain't criers. They're brought up not to show their emotions, and no matter what happens they don't cry."

"But you cried at the hospital when I had my appendix out."

"I'm different, ain't I?"

"Yes, you're a pussy cat."

Nathan hugged me as he put his lips together and softly murmured, "Meow."

CHAPTER 9

The following morning Nathan and I sat in the rented brand new 1966 Cadillac across the street from Miss Sophia's Beauty Academy. I breathed in the unmistakable fresh odor of the black leather and it smelled like perfume to me. The air-conditioner kept us comfortable, while outside the August sun blazed, resulting in steamy, thick air. If a hen was outside, it could lay a hard-boiled egg. Nathan was right when he insisted we rent a car. There wasn't even a breeze to cause the fronds on the palm trees to sway. We waited a half-hour until Angela left the school accompanied by Ricardo.

*　　*　　*

Detectives Lenhart and Gaspard, in an unmarked car, followed Sadie and Nathan's Cadillac. Lenhart felt in his gut if he followed the nutty woman she would reveal herself as Dolly's killer. She would make a grave mistake and he would catch her.

Julie reached into her pocket for a slice of Juicy Fruit gum. She was the kind of woman whose mouth always had to be engaged. If she wasn't talking, she was chewing, biting down like a bear on a salmon.

Lenhart drove slowly. "It would be easier if the murderer used a gun or a knife or even a rolling pin. Someone who uses poison is always harder to catch."

"We'll catch her," Gaspard said as she stuck another slice of gum in her mouth.

"I know we will. We've solved many murders, and the criminal always gives away his or her hand. It's just a matter of patience and time."

*   *   *

Like a hawk, I watched Angela and Ricardo turn the corner before Nathan started the car. As they strode down the block, we followed closely but at a safe distance. The block was empty of people who knew better than to walk in the torturous summer heat.

Both students went into Julio's Hispanic Grocery. It took twenty minutes before Ricardo came out with shopping bags piled high.

I squirmed in my seat, crunching down so my suspect, Angela, wouldn't see me. Nathan drove slowly and parked when Ricardo and Angela went into a bungalow that had a yard filled with flowering bushes. We waited to see if they would come out. Meanwhile, Nathan snoozed in the driver's seat. I always said he could sleep even if he had been in bed in the 1906 San Francisco earthquake.

I crossed my legs, then uncrossed them, then crossed them again and picked at a hangnail. Adrenaline cruised through my body and I had to do something fast before I screamed with frustration. Opening the door, I crawled out. The bungalow had the venetians in the front window partially opened. Scrunched over, I moved to the window and peered in through a slat.

Angela and Ricardo were watching a soap opera on TV.

This was getting me nowhere.

*　　*　　*

Returning to the car, I slipped into the passenger's seat next to Nathan who woke up. "Well, have you learned anything yet?"

"Yes. Angela and Ricardo must be married or lovers. They live in the same place and I think both of them were involved in Dolly's murder."

Suddenly Detective Lenhart knocked on the window on the driver's side. Nathan grabbed the handle and rolled down the window.

"You've been following us," I said, annoyance in my voice.

The detective's eyes glared with anger. "You bet. Ever since you two left the hotel I've been on your tail."

"You should be doing your job and not watching an innocent person like me." I pointed my index finger at him. "Angela and Ricardo are the ones you should be suspicious of, not me. They live together and are lovers."

Detective Lenhart grimaced. "You think you know something important, but you don't. Angela and Ricardo are fraternal twins. He went to a special school in Columbia where he learned English. Angela refused to go. Their wealthy father sent them to America with the idea of their going into the beauty school business back in Columbia. Mrs. Weinstein, I'll warn you only once; don't follow anyone or I'll arrest you for interfering with a murder investigation."

"But Detective, can't you figure out that they come from Columbia and the poison-dart frog also comes from Columbia? You put two and two together and you get the murderers."

"Get out of the car, both of you, right now."

With no choice, we opened the doors and stepped out.

"I'm arresting you, Mrs. Weinstein. Put your hands behind your back so I can cuff you."

I sighed as I held out my hands and in an instant cold steel cuffs clicked into place on my wrists. "Oy, they're tight. You just told me that you wouldn't arrest me and now you go back on your word and that's unfair. I'll report you to the higher-ups."

"You said something to implicate yourself." The detective turned to me and pulled a card out of his pocket. "This is a U.S. law that was just passed following the 1966 *Miranda v. Arizona* Supreme Court decision and now I will read you the Miranda warning. 'You have the right to remain silent. Anything you say or do may be used against you in a court of law. You have the right to consult an attorney."

"I don't need an attorney." The perspiration flowed down my face both from the heat and the aggravation.

"Don't interrupt me. 'If you cannot afford an attorney, one will be appointed for you.' Do you understand what I just read to you?"

"Sure I understand. I'm no dummy. I don't want a lawyer." Taking a deep breath of the hot, moist air, I shouted, "I'm innocent, I tell you!"

I was stuffed like a bag of garbage into the back of their car.

After we reached the police station, a two-story, red-bricked building, Nathan sat in the outer room when I was booked. When the cuffs were removed, I massaged my wrists. I wriggled as my fingerprints were taken. I complained that I needed to comb my hair when my picture was snapped and made sure to smile even though the officer told me not to.

Finally, I was led to a room with no windows, three metal chairs, and a table with a recording device that Detective Lenhart turned on.

"Sit," he ordered.

I took the seat across from him and tapped my index finger on the table making a sound like the tapping of a woodpecker. I wondered what I had said that made him haul me in.

I wriggled on the chair in the police station while I appealed to Detective Lenhart. "I changed my mind. I need a lawyer. You said I could have a lawyer for free."

"We'll send for one," Gaspard said.

I sat uncomfortably on the chair wondering why I was arrested. *Will I land in jail? Will I be convicted of a crime I never committed?*

A half-hour later Lenhart said, "Your lawyer is on his way."

I twisted and twisted on my chair. "I have to go to the bathroom." I didn't have to go, but I felt suffocated in the interrogation room.

"Hold it in. Your attorney is coming any minute."

Lenhart had a mean expression and I wasn't going to argue.

A couple of minutes later, a tall man shaped like a bread stick, came in. He looked to me like he had just graduated from high school and had never made it to law school. With a vacant expression in his cat green eyes, he didn't appeal to me, and I wondered if there was a brain in his head. When something is free, I'm always suspicious.

"My name is Peter Cameron and I'll represent you."

"I'm innocent."

"Everyone says that. It makes no difference to me if you're innocent or guilty. I'll see that you get a fair trial."

"Oh, my God, I'm going to trial."

The young attorney's face was so smooth it looked as if he had never shaved in his life. "Mrs. Weinstein, anything that you say to me is strictly confidential."

"Did you learn that in law school?"

"As a matter of fact, I did."

"I don't believe it."

Cameron took a handkerchief from the pocket of his trousers and blew his nose.

For two minutes we sat looking at each other. I didn't know if I could trust him. I tapped my foot until he looked down at it and I stopped.

Finally I said, "Take me outside and I'll tell you what I know."

He nodded. We walked through a long corridor and sat down on a bench in the outer room of the police station. Groups of cops were talking loudly. One cop had cuffs on a guy who had a torn straw hat on his head and looked like a bum.

"No one is eavesdropping. You can tell me everything you know." Cameron took a small notebook and a pen from his jacket pocket.

"I don't want you to write this down."

"No one will see it," he said.

"I don't care. I won't speak until you put the notebook away."

The attorney moved the notebook from one hand to the other like he was playing ball. I think he would've been more comfortable on a tennis court than in this crowded police station. He looked like he was deciding where he would go on vacation before he tucked the notebook and the pen back in his pocket.

"All right, I'll open up. I was there when Ricardo, a student at the beauty school, was going to wash Dolly's hair. Someone stuck her with a poison dart, and I know it wasn't me. I started thinking it might be Angela, but I wanted to know what kind of poison it was, so . . . ."

The attorney interrupted me. "Why was it your business to find out? Why couldn't you leave the investigating to the police?"

"Look, you may not believe me, but I went to the morgue and waited until someone came out. The first woman wouldn't talk to me, but the second man did."

"Very interesting," Cameron said. "Just how did you get him to talk?"

"I'm a good liar, and I said I was writing a mystery and I needed to know what a morgue looked like."

"Couldn't you ring the bell and ask to be shown around?"

"I was sure that wouldn't work. Who would show a stranger around a morgue? You don't understand. It wasn't that I wanted to see a morgue. No, who wants to see dead people get cut up? I wanted to know about Dolly's autopsy and what they found."

Cameron leaned forward and looked really interested. I went on with my explanation. "I was lucky that the man who came out seemed to be attracted to me. He invited me to lunch and I went with him. Then, after we ate and he told me he was the medical examiner, I asked him to tell me about one of his interesting cases."

"Did he fall for that?"

"You bet he did. He told me that this lady, who died in a beauty school, had been injected with the venom of the poison-dart frog, and that's the truth."

Cameron, unexpectedly, tapped me on my shoulder. "I think you invented this story, but I will still represent you. Now do you think you can tell me the truth? If you killed Dolly, you must have a good reason."

"I'm finished talking to you."

CHAPTER 10

Detective Lenhart straightened his tie. "You claim you're not guilty in the Morris case," he said in a manly baritone.

"Morris case?"

"Sorry, Mrs. Weinstein. I don't mean to be disrespectful. I should have said — in your friend's murder."

"Poor Dolly," I said quietly.

"You did admit it was your fault."

"I already explained why, when I told you if it wasn't for my going to Miami Beach, Dolly would've remained in Brooklyn and she still would be alive."

"There's a way to help clear you. It's not completely reliable, but it's a step in the right direction. It's called a polygraph test and it has some utility. It's completely voluntary. In the event that it's entered into evidence in a trial, then it's subject to the discretion of the trial judge. I can't force you to take this test, Mrs. Weinstein."

I sat back and weighed my chances. I know about lie detector tests from what I had seen in the movies and on TV. Maybe, if I take the test, the idiot wouldn't bother me anymore and I can proceed with my own investigation. "I volunteer to take the lie detector test."

*　　*　　*

The temperature in Miami was 92° with high humidity, but the polygraph room was air-conditioned making my skin crawl with goosebumps. The handsome examiner, dressed in a white lab coat over tan slacks, introduced himself as Dr. Whitney. He gave me a gentle smile, and seated me in a chair next to a table that had a machine with threatening wires and knobs.

Dr. Whitney explained that the wires were for measuring and recording several physiological signs such as pulse, blood pressure, respiration, and skin conductivity. He said calmly, "All the time that you're hooked up, I'll ask you a series of questions that you'll answer." He looked me straight in my eyes and added, "Deceptive answers will produce physiological responses that I'll be able to discern as lies, so it is important for you to answer truthfully. Do you understand what I just told you?"

"Yes, sir, I understand." He must think I'm a moron, I thought.

Dr. Whitney attached electrodes to different parts of my body and asked if I was comfortable. I was afraid to lie so I told the truth. "I'm scared. I never had one of these tests. Does it hurt?"

"Just relax. I assure you there is no pain involved. It won't take long. Now I'll ask you a question and you are to deliberately lie so I can monitor your physical response."

"Hold off, Dr. Whitney. I'm not a good liar."

Actually, I just lied because when it comes to lying I can win first prize, but I wasn't going to reveal that fact.

"Just do the best that you can. What is your name?"

"Gregory Peck."

"That was good. I was able to detect that you lied. From now on answer the questions truthfully."

"Yes, sir."

"What is your name?"

"Sadie Chaya Weinstein."

"Where do you live?"

"I live in a four-room apartment on the third floor of an apartment house at 315 Lenox Road in Flatbush. That's a neighborhood in Brooklyn, New York? How am I doing?"

"Fine. Your answers don't have to be that involved. How do you feel about the death of Dolly Morris?"

I decided to give him one word answers. "Awful."

"Do you have anything that might injure a person?"

"Yes."

"What?"

"A rolling pin."

"Are you a violent person?"

"What do you mean by violent?"

"No, Mrs. Weinstein. I ask the questions, not you."

"Okay."

"Let's try this again. Are you easily angered?"

"I'm getting there."

"Have you been known to kill within the last week?"

"Yes."

"Did you kill Dolly Morris?"

"No."

"Who did you kill?"

"A big bug on the kitchen counter in my hotel."

"Thank you, Mrs. Weinstein. That's all for now, except that your husband left a message that he was hungry and went back to the hotel."

*   *   *

Dr. Whitney sat at Detective Lenhart's desk with a report of the polygraph test. The detective held up his hand, "I have no time to read your report, just tell me if Weinstein killed Morris?"

"In all the twenty years I've practiced, I never met a woman like that."

"Don't beat around the bush. Is she the perp?"

"She's not only not a perpetrator, she's flaky."

"Could she have been faking it?" The detective wrinkled his brow.

"If she was, she did a brilliant job. Whether she screwed it up deliberately or not, I can't say, but she's the most eccentric person I ever tested. She blew me away."

CHAPTER 11

At 4 p.m. I was released from the police station where I had been unjustly accused of Dolly's murder and detained for many annoying hours taking the polygraph test.

It would be close to closing time at the morgue and I decided to grab a cab and wait until Dr. Lucas Porter left. I leaned against a tall palm tree and spent only a few minutes until the small man with the thick glasses came through the door. Gingerly, I approached him.

"Hi, Dr. Porter."

"Oh, hello pretty lady. I didn't think I'd ever see you again. You couldn't resist my charm, could you?"

"I need to talk to you."

"Okay. Let's go back to the restaurant where we were before. We can sit in the same booth and get reacquainted."

"All right. I'm not hungry, so I won't have anything but a glass of water."

"You're a cheap date."

Lucas smiled broadly, his incisor with its gold inlay glittering. Feeling like a lowdown fraud, I was compelled to tell the truth which made me grit my teeth in anticipation of anxiety.

I had to set him straight. "This is not a date."

"Then why do you want to talk to me?"

"Let me just say I need to confess something as my conscience is killing me."

Behind his thick-lensed spectacles, Lucas opened his eyes wide. "Ohhh, this is going to be interesting. Let's get a move on."

Lucas led me to the same booth we had occupied before. He ordered a hamburger with a side of cole slaw and a cup of coffee.

"Are you sure you don't want anything?" he asked.

"No, thanks. I'm good."

"We have time until my food comes, so why don't you reveal your little secret?"

I had my hand on the formica table and he covered my hand with his. His fingers were long for a short man and I noticed his nails were clean. In an awkward way, I pulled my hand from his and rested it on my lap.

I took a breath as deep as the lake in Prospect Park. "My name isn't Sandra Weinberg. It's Sadie Weinstein. I'm not an author. I read mysteries but I don't write them."

"Really? I should have known that a woman as attractive as you wouldn't go for a man like me." Lucas opened his dark eyes wide. "So why did you lie to me?"

I took a sip of the ice water. Then I took another sip trying to delay my embarrassing confession. "Well, you see. I'm not exactly a regular detective. I own a grocery. Dolly Morris asked me to go with her to Miami Beach and she wound up murdered in the beauty school. I lied to you because I wanted to know what killed her. I don't have confidence in the police here and I want to solve this murder."

Dr. Porter bit down on his lips.

I continued, "I was arrested when I let it slip to the detectives that Dolly was killed with the venom of the poison-dart frog. I don't know why they let me out, but I thought my lawyer told them who I got the information from, and I was scared that you'd be fired."

Lucas's jaw dropped. "No one told me about this."

"I was sure it was the lawyer who told them."

"Where did you reveal the information?"

Twisting in my seat, I lowered my wavering voice. "In the outer room in the police station."

Lucas guffawed. "The whole police station is bugged. It's nice of you to be concerned about my welfare, but they'd never fire me even if they knew I gave you that information. I told you I'm the best medical examiner in these United States. I admire your guts and maybe we can have a serious relationship."

"That's out of the question."

From out of nowhere, Nathan appeared. He put his hand on my shoulder. I shuddered. *What was he doing here?* "Did you follow me from the police station?" I hadn't told Lucas yet that I was married and now I was falling down a well of my own making.

Lucas pointed his hairy finger at Nathan. "Who is this rude man?"

Nathan ignored him. Angrily, he turned to me. "Yeah, I followed you to keep you from getting into hot water and here you are in a restaurant with a strange man, and a strange-looking man at that."

"I can explain," I said shaking from head to toe.

Nathan ignored me. He looked like he was about to murder Lucas. "I'm Sadie's husband and you are a good-for-nothing wife stealer, you Lothario, you Don Juan, you pig. You better keep away from my wife or else." Nathan fisted his hand and I trembled.

"Or else what?" Lucas asked with a puzzled expression.

"Calm down, Nathan," I whispered, trying to control a scene that was quickly getting out of hand. "Why did you follow me?" I repeated.

"I wanted to see what you were up to. Are you in the habit of going into a restaurant with a man?"

"No. Let me introduce you. Nathan Weinstein this is Dr. Lucas Porter, the medical examiner, the one who did the autopsy on Dolly."

Nathan looked chagrined. He held out his hand. Lucas wiped his hands on his napkin, and shook hands with Nathan.

"Why didn't you tell me you were married?" Lucas asked in exasperation.

"The first time we met I took off my wedding ring. I believed if you thought I was single, you'd be more likely to open up. But this time I kept my wedding ring on. Didn't you notice it?"

The ice in the glass was melting and I desperately needed another sip of water.

I had dug a hole as deep as a trench. Now both men would never trust me again.

CHAPTER 12

"Nathan, let's go back to our room. I have some thinking to do."

Nathan bit down on his lips. "You've been thinking too much. Thinking is getting you into hot water. You need a nap and so do I."

We got in the car and drove back to our hotel. Nathan was right. I was exhausted and, after I took off my dress, I lay down on the bed and fell into a troubled sleep. I dreamed about Dolly and how she was sitting in the office of her psychiatrist talking to her, motioning wildly with her hands."

I woke up, dressed quietly while Nathan kept snoring, sprawled out on the bedspread, and looking dead to the world. I went down to the lobby and entered the library section next to the restaurant. I needed the time to ponder what my next step would be.

Seated on the armchair, I began to entertain the thought that perhaps, when I looked away, Dolly had taken the dart or needle or whatever it was that was used to inject the poison, and stuck herself. But where had she obtained the poison? Maybe somehow she managed. It could be she really was intent on suicide.

I dialed the hotel phone and asked the long distance operator to look for Dr. Shelly Ferguson's number in Manhattan. Dr. Ferguson had first treated Dolly when she attempted to commit suicide after the death of her only child, and Dolly had continued to see her.

Charging the call to my room, luckily I reached the psychiatrist.

"My name is Mrs. Sadie Weinstein and I'm a friend of Dolly Morris. Doctor Ferguson, I'm sorry to tell you that Dolly died from the injection of venom from the poison-dart frog. I know she was your patient and that she tried to commit suicide once before. In the light of her past history, do you think there's a possibility she killed herself now? Had she spoken recently about committing suicide? Just how depressed was she? Was she on any medication that would have caused her to commit suicide?"

"Mrs. Weinstein, I'm sorry to hear about the untimely death of Mrs. Morris. Due to confidentiality, I can't tell you any more than that."

She hung up and I was frustrated the way Nathan feels when *The New York Times* puzzle asks about pop singers he knows nothing about.

Okay, supposing Dolly did commit suicide, does that mean I shouldn't act like it wasn't murder? Deep down I knew that Dolly was depressed, but she was healing and wouldn't take her life at this point. I would continue with my investigation. I had no choice.

CHAPTER 13

I took the elevator back to our room and brewed a cup of coffee. Nathan heard the popping sound and woke up.

"I have to continue the investigation, Nathan."

"Not without me, you won't," Nathan said as he sat on the bed.

"Of course with you. Let's see what can happen if we follow Angela again."

Nathan perked up. "Why Angela? Do you think there's a chance that Ricardo killed Dolly?"

I thought over the possibility. "Who knows? Maybe. Maybe not. He stood right over her. That's why we'll wait for him to leave the beauty academy. Maybe he and Angela planned it."

"Why?"

"I don't know, but it could be they were paid killers."

Nathan shook his head. "Have you considered that Miss Sophia could be the killer?"

"I don't think so."

"Why not?"

"This is her academy, and when and if there's a murder there, she loses business. People get scared and go someplace else. No, Nathan, I don't think she did it."

When we pulled into the hotel's parking lot, we saw Don scurry toward the beauty academy. I noticed he wasn't lugging his valise filled with the merchandise he sells. "Nathan, I wonder why Don is going to the beauty school."

"Maybe he's getting a massage. Maybe he needs a haircut."

I shook my head. "I don't think so. Park the car and let's see when he comes out."

We waited ten minutes before Don and Miss Sophia exited. They were talking animatedly right before they stepped into a Buick on the other side of the parking lot.

"We'll follow them," I said. "Start the motor and keep back so they don't see us."

I fastened my eyes on the car in front of us, all the while telling Nathan to keep back.

We drove about twenty-five minutes before Don parked the car. We kept out of sight and watched while Don and Miss Sophia stood in front of a large luxurious ranch house with a sign that read "For Sale." A young woman wearing a pink linen dress stepped out of the house, and motioned for them to enter.

"This is very suspicious," I said. I took out a pad and pen from my purse and jotted down the address.

"Maybe not," Nathan said. "It could be that Don knows Miss Sophia because he sold her cosmetic products and he's helping her buy a house."

I opened my eyes wide. "I don't think so. I bet they're planning to move in together. I'm changing my mind about Angela and Ricardo. I think these two are in league and it was Miss Sophia who killed Dolly."

"Even if it was, how are you going to prove it?"

"Nathan, I remember when Dolly told me that Don had traveled to many countries she named them. And I think she said one of them was Columbia. I want to make sure before I go any further."

Nathan pulled a handkerchief from his pants pocket and blew his nose. The sound was deafening. "And how will you make sure?"

"I'll sneak into his room and look for his passport. I bet he doesn't take it with him."

"And if he ain't got a passport, what will you do?"

"When we checked in at the airport, we showed our driver's license, and he pulled out his passport."

"Okay, Sadie, you see everything. But why didn't you see who stuck Dolly?"

"It happened too fast. And, believe me I feel miserable I didn't notice."

*　　*　　*

As we were driving back to the hotel, I asked Nathan to stop in front of a candy store. I went in and bought a big box of Schrafft's chocolates.

When I paid for the box, I said to the clerk with the Charlie Chaplin moustache, "I don't need a bag, just a pretty blue ribbon on top of the box."

As Nathan drove the car, I had the box on my lap. "Why did you buy candy?" he asked. "Is it for me?"

"You'll see," I said. "I love you, but I didn't buy it for you."

"You have a secret lover?" Nathan screwed up his face.

"That statement doesn't require an answer," I said.

Luckily, after we returned to the hotel, the young maid with braids was making up our room. I held up the box of chocolates. "Please, can you do me a favor?" I asked with a smile. "Will you please open the room next door so I can leave this box for my brother? It's his birthday."

She stopped making our bed, and rushed to open the door of Don's room.

"Thank you," I said.

In the corridor Nathan said, "Sadie, you're a genius."

"Sometimes, Nathan, I dazzle myself."

Nathan and I stepped in. I went to the desk and opened the drawer. The passport wasn't there.

In the top drawer of the dresser, underneath Don's boxers, Nathan found the passport. Hurriedly, he looked through it and held it up for me to see. It was stamped with the seal of Columbia and dated last year.

I started to rummage through all the drawers and in the bottom drawer I found a photo of Don and Miss Sophia at the beach. Both were smiling, arms around each other, dressed in bathing suits. I held it up for Nathan to see. He whistled.

I left the candy on the desk. We took the elevator to the lobby and sat on the sofa until we saw Don enter a half-hour later. He looked happy, not like a man who had just lost his wife. As he stood waiting for the elevator, I approached him. "Hi, Don. Nathan and I were just going out for a bite. Would you like to join us?"

Don paused. "Thanks, but no thanks, Sadie. I just had a bite in a coffee shop in Miami."

"Miami?" Nathan said.

"Yes, I was showing my samples to a beauty parlor there."

"Did they order anything?" I asked.

"Sure. They ordered ten wigs and lots of other beauty supplies. Here's the elevator. Are you going up?"

"Not yet," I said. "Nathan and I are going for a walk around the lake. See you later." I hesitated while Don had his hand above the elevator button. "By the way, I bought you a box of candy and the maid brought it to your room. I thought that your grief would be somewhat assuaged by sweets."

"Thanks, Sadie. That was thoughtful of you," Don pressed the elevator button and the door opened. "So long for now," he said as he entered the elevator.

"We're going for a walk?" Nathan asked.

"Yeah. Let's walk around the lake and talk."

We went outside. The temperature was a little lower but the humidity was still high. We strolled along the cobblestoned walkway, quickly passing the spot where the mother swan was still sitting on her nest.

"It's obvious he's lying," I said. "He didn't see us when he entered the house with Miss Sophia."

"What do we do now?" Nathan asked.

"Now we find a real estate agent and tell her we're interested in buying the house that Don and Miss Sophia looked at."

"Why?" Nathan asked.

"Because we have to find out if they're buying that house, and, if so, who is buying it? Don? Miss Sophia? Both of them?"

"You're so smart."

"Thank you. And you're so cute." We continued walking around the lake holding hands.

"Here's what I speculate," I said. "Don knew Miss Sophia for a few years. She's pretty and rich and Dolly was not taking care of herself. It must've been hard for him to be married to a depressed person."

Nathan shrugged.

"Anyway, when he went to Columbia, somehow he got hold of the venom and brought it back to Florida and told Miss Sophia to hold on to it. Then he persuaded Dolly to go to Miami Beach, only she wouldn't unless we went along. Together they came up with the plan for Miss Sophia to kill Dolly with the venom. It was a good plan, except that I saw through the evil plot."

"Okay, Sadie, how are you going to prove that it was Miss Sophia who used the poison?"

"I don't know. I have to think about it. The circumstantial evidence we found won't hold up."

That night as I tossed in bed, the sheets curled around my legs like a boa constrictor. Both drinking a glass of milk and reading weren't as soporific as I had imagined. I awoke at 3 a.m. after dreaming about Miss Sophia, dressed in a devil's outfit, leaning over Dolly, sticking her with a needle.

I poked Nathan who woke up kvetching. "Oy!"

"I have a plan. First, we go to the real estate agent and find out about the house. Second, we go to the beauty academy and I look for the needle with the venom. What do you think?"

"I think I want to go back to sleep."

"All right, but I'll wake you early in the morning."

I tried to go back to sleep, but no go until 5 a.m.

That morning Nathan had gotten up before me. I heard the shower pinging in the bathroom. My eyes burned from lack of sleep, but I got up anyway. This was going to be an eventful day, the day when Dolly's murderers would pay for their crime.

We were in luck when we found the closest real estate office near the house that the evil couple had looked at. It was a store front between a vet and a barber shop. When we entered, we met a woman with heavy makeup.

"Good morning," I said. "My husband and I saw a house near here that we'd like to look at. The address is 519 Laurel Drive. Yesterday it had a For Sale sign, but today the sign has been removed. Does that mean it's no longer available?"

"I'm sorry, but a couple has given us a down payment on that address. However, we have many other wonderful homes for you to examine."

I moved toward the door. "No, thank you. We had our hearts set on that one. Let's go, Howard." I took Nathan's hand and pulled him out the door.

In the car I told Nathan my second plan. "Let's speculate that Miss Sophia stuck Dolly with the needle and had to get rid of it in a hurry. She raced to her office and called 911, and she must've put it someplace where she thought the police wouldn't find it which I assume they haven't. I bet it's somewhere in her desk. The police aren't looking for it because they're sure I killed Dolly."

"It's too dangerous for you to go looking for it. I nix it."

It's sweet of Nathan to care about my safety, and to tell the truth, I'm scared, but I'll never admit it. "I hear you, but I'm going through with it, that is if I have your help."

"I ain't getting involved with such a hairbrained scheme."

I put my hand on Nathan's shoulder and left it there. I had to appeal to his sense of duty. "Look, dear, if we succeed with this plan, I'll be off the hook, the murderers will suffer, and we can go home and take care of our grocery."

"You're an impossible yenta."

"I know. Now will you help me?"

Nathan reached into the glove compartment for a tissue that he grabbed. He wiped the sweat under his eyes. "What's your plan?"

"You go to the beauty academy for a massage."

Nathan wrinkled his forehead. "Sadie, I ain't getting no massage. No woman, but you, will put her hands on me. I won't do it."

"I understand. That's very loyal of you. But you can ask for a male masseuse."

"I hate having my body rubbed."

"It's the only way for me to be safe." I hoped I could get through to him.

"I ain't sure about this."

"When you're getting the massage, you scream. Everyone will rush to your side while I sneak into Miss Sophia's office and go through her desk."

Nathan looked at me like I was crazy. He shook his head. "Suppose Miss Sophia sees you and she kills you. No. I won't take such a chance."

"All right. I'll call the police and warn them what I plan to do. Then you get your massage. I just know I'll find the poisoned needle."

Nathan scratched his head and frowned. "Suppose you don't, they'll re-arrest you."

"We have to chance it. Please, Nathan, let's do it."

Nathan was silent. He looked like he was about to get a migraine. "You'll be careful not to stick yourself if you find it?"

"Of course." I wasn't so sure about this, but I had no choice but to lie.

"Okay." Nathan wiped the sweat from his brow.

I raced to the hotel and found the closest phone. My fingers were trembling when I called Detective Lenhart.

"This is Sadie Weinstein. Don't say anything. Just listen. I'm going to the beauty academy and I'm searching for the needle with the venom. Come immediately."

When he started to scream, I hung up, ran back to the beauty academy, and sent Nathan in for a massage.

I stood outside in the boiling sun and waited ten minutes. My blouse was sticking to my back and sweat was pouring down my face. When Nathan screamed so loudly you could've heard him in Coney Island, I ran into the reception area. Gorgeous had already left. No one was around.

I bolted across the room and rushed into Miss Sophia's office. With trembling hands, I opened the top drawer.

The police siren outside wailed. I shook from fright, but in the drawer I found an appointment book, four #2 pencils, two Bic pens, and a fat pen that looked like it might have the needle in it. My hands trembled as I opened the book and looked at the entry for Tuesday, *Don, lunch, our house.* The phone rang, startling me, but I didn't answer it. Instead I opened the fountain pen and jumped for joy when I found the cartridge was missing, but the needle was inside a tube in the pen. I had hit the jackpot.

Suddenly Miss Sophia burst into the office. "You miserable excuse for a woman," she cried with a cockney accent, as she saw her desk drawer open and, in my hand, the pen with the tube in it. She ran to the desk and grabbed a letter opener shaped like a dagger, the sharp point facing me. She attempted to stab me, but I avoided her by running around the desk. She tried to grab me, but I was too agile for her. We raced in a circle around the desk, her hand held high, menacing me with the letter opener.

As I ran away from her, I stumbled and fell over the leg of the desk chair. I felt myself dropping down in slow motion. I tried to hang on to the desk, but I couldn't grab it. Miss Sophia stood over me, her face a twisted grotesque mask, her hand holding the deadly weapon, pointing it at my neck. Her intention was to stab my carotid artery causing me to bleed to death.

My adrenaline rose to its highest level. I twisted away.

Miss Sophia glared. "You can't get away from me, you piece of vermin."

I shouted, "You murdered Dolly. You're lower than vermin."

Jumping up, I ran to the door and put my hand on the knob to open it, as she followed me and tried to pierce my skin. I pushed her away with all my strength and as I opened the door, Detective Lenhart and Detective Gaspard burst in, guns drawn.

"Throw down the dagger," the detective shouted.

When Miss Sophia saw the guns pointed at her, she complied.

I stood up and planted a kiss on Detective Lenhart's cheek. "Here's proof," I cried as I bent down and picked up the pen holding it away from my body, "that Don Morris and Miss Sophia plotted Dolly's murder, and Miss Sophia executed it."

Suddenly Nathan stepped in, barefoot, his chest hairs covered with oil, a towel around his belly that he held up with both hands. He cocked his head, narrowed his dark Hershey chocolate eyes, and snapped, "Can't you see my wife is holding a pen with the poisoned needle?"

"Sure, we see it," Detective Lenhart said. "So what? She put it there."

I was so incensed I stamped my foot. I wanted to take back the kiss I had given him. "I did not!" I protested. It was Miss Sophia who called 911 when Dolly collapsed. She hid the needle in the pen."

"Maybe. We'll have to have it tested for the poison," Detective Lenhart said impatiently. Then he fixed his eyes on Nathan, who swallowed hard. "Why are you undressed?"

Nathan's mouth quivered slightly. "I was having a massage."

"You people are the strangest couple I have ever met."

"No," I contradicted. "If you're looking for a strange couple, look at Miss Sophia and Don Morris. Their warped minds are filled with psychological bacteria. She just tried to stab me. She would've killed me if you hadn't stopped her." I picked up the notebook and shoved it in front of Detective Lenhart's eyes. "You see they are a couple. They bought a house and planned the horrendous murder together thinking they could get away with it."

Detective Gaspard moved next to her partner and whispered something in his ear. I tried to hear but she spoke too low.

Detective Lenhart slipped the handcuffs on Miss Sophia and led her out the door.

I looked at Nathan and smiled.

He said, "As soon as my massage is over, we're going out and celebrating."

I nodded. I was so happy I felt like downing a hot fudge sundae with whipped cream topped with a cherry.

*   *   *

After the medical examiner tested the venom and it proved positive, Nathan and I took a plane home.

At the trial the prosecutor exposed the fact that Don had a life insurance policy for one million dollars on Dolly's life.

Don and Miss Sophia were sent to prison for seventy-five years for the murder of Dolly Morris. And I needed another vacation but had to go back to waiting on customers in our grocery.

Next year, for sure we're going to the Grand Canyon.